Dear Parents:

Congratulations! Your child is taking the first steps on an exciting journey. The destination? Independent reading!

STEP INTO READING® will help your child get there. The program offers five steps to reading success. Each step includes fun stories and colorful art or photographs. In addition to original fiction and books with favorite characters, there are Step into Reading Non-Fiction Readers, Phonics Readers and Boxed Sets, Sticker Readers, and Comic Readers—a complete literacy program with something to interest every child.

Learning to Read, Step by Step!

Ready to Read Preschool–Kindergarten
• big type and easy words • rhyme and rhythm • picture clues
For children who know the alphabet and are eager to begin reading.

Reading with Help Preschool–Grade 1
• basic vocabulary • short sentences • simple stories
For children who recognize familiar words and sound out new words with help.

Reading on Your Own Grades 1–3
• engaging characters • easy-to-follow plots • popular topics
For children who are ready to read on their own.

Reading Paragraphs Grades 2–3
• challenging vocabulary • short paragraphs • exciting stories
For newly independent readers who read simple sentences with confidence.

Ready for Chapters Grades 2–4
• chapters • longer paragraphs • full-color art
For children who want to take the plunge into chapter books but still like colorful pictures.

STEP INTO READING® is designed to give every child a successful reading experience. The grade levels are only guides; children will progress through the steps at their own speed, developing confidence in their reading.

Remember, a lifetime love of reading starts with a single step!

Visit us on the Web!
StepIntoReading.com
rhcbooks.com

Educators and librarians, for a variety of teaching tools, visit us at RHTeachersLibrarians.com

ISBN 978-0-525-57812-3 (trade) — ISBN 978-0-525-57813-0 (lib. bdg.)

Printed in the United States of America   10 9 8 7 6 5 4 3 2 1

nickelodeon

I L♥VE QUEEN MOM!

Nella THE PRINCESS KNIGHT

WITHDRAWN

adapted by Tex Huntley

based on the teleplay "A Royally Awesome Beach Day"
by Lucas Mills

illustrated by Nneka Myers

Random House 🏠 New York

Queen Mom is
Nella the Princess
Knight's mother.

Queen Mom loves Nella.

She loves

Princess Norma, too.

The busy day begins.

Queen Mom and the girls
eat pancakes.
Yum!

Nella loves to play
games with Queen Mom.
After breakfast,
they play gobletball.

Queen Mom is really good!

Later, Nella dances
in a show.

Queen Mom proudly
cheers for Nella.
Clap! Clap! Clap!

It is time for
a royal tea party.

Queen Mom serves fruit.

Nella pours tea.

Next, they go
on an adventure
to the beach.

Queen Mom pulls
Princess Norma
in a red wagon.

Oh, no!
Snorklemanders!

They splash!

They throw a green ball.

The ball will hit Norma!

Can someone stop it?

Nella becomes
a Princess Knight!

Queen Mom holds
Princess Norma.
Nella stops the ball!

Nella asks
the snorklemanders
to play nicely.
The beach adventure
is saved!

The busy day is over.

Queen Mom always
has time for
a bedtime story.

Nella loves Queen Mom!